Seaponies
Make a Splash!

Adapted by Bonnie Ventura
Based on the original screenplay "My Little Pony: The Movie"
by Rita Hsiao, Meghan McCarthy, and Michael Vogel

Illustrated by Drake Brodahl

 A GOLDEN BOOK • NEW YORK

Licensed by:

Hasbro

HASBRO and its logo, MY LITTLE PONY, and all related characters are trademarks of Hasbro
and are used with permission. © 2017 Hasbro. All Rights Reserved. MY LITTLE PONY: THE MOVIE © 2017
My Little Pony Productions, LLC.

Published in the United States by Golden Books, an imprint of Random House Children's Books, a division of
Penguin Random House LLC, 1745 Broadway, New York, NY 10019, and in Canada by Penguin Random House
Canada Limited, Toronto. Golden Books, A Golden Book, A Big Golden Book, the G colophon, and the distinctive
gold spine are registered trademarks of Penguin Random House LLC.

rhcbooks.com

ISBN 978-1-5247-6964-2 (trade) — ISBN 978-1-5247-6965-9 (ebook)

Printed in the United States of America

10 9 8 7 6 5 4 3 2 1

Princess Twilight Sparkle, Pinkie Pie, Rainbow Dash, Applejack, Fluttershy, Rarity, and Spike are on an adventure. They're exploring a strange underwater kingdom far from their home. After spying a friendly Seapony, they follow her into the mysterious deep.

The Seapony's name is Skystar. The friends soon discover that she is not just *any* Seapony. **She's a princess!**

Princess Skystar is so excited to have guests! She takes her new friends to meet her mother. The group swims through a village full of Seaponies before they arrive at a magnificent underwater castle.

Queen Novo doesn't know if she should trust the surface dwellers. Just as she is about to signal for her guards, Princess Skystar tells her mother the ponies are her friends.

Princess Twilight Sparkle has so many questions for her hosts. Princess Skystar decides to answer them by telling a story.

"Once upon a time, Hippogriffs—part ponies, part eagles—lived on a big mountain," Skystar explains.

"One day, the Storm King came to steal their magic, so their brave and majestic leader, Queen Novo, led her subjects deep underwater where the beast could never go," she continues.

"We are the Hippogriffs! **Ta-da!**" Skystar cheers.

"Hold on. Let me get this straight," Applejack says.
"When the Storm King came, you ran?"

"We didn't run, we swam!" Skystar answers.
"But how?" Twilight Sparkle asks.

Queen Novo swims above her throne. She taps a
jellyfish, which opens to reveal the most beautiful pearl
anypony has ever seen, and places her hooves on it.
A bright white light fills the throne room. Suddenly,
a magical force swirls around the guests . . .

. . . and turns them all into Seaponies!

"These fins are divine!" Rarity exclaims.

"Hey, Applejack! I'll race you to that coral!"
Rainbow Dash shouts.

"You're on!" Applejack hollers.

Pinkie Pie uses her new fins to spin around in the water. "**Woo-hoo!** Try it, Fluttershy!" she encourages her friend.

Fluttershy does a small spin. "Yay!" she giggles.

"Guys! What's happening?" Spike squeals.
He floats off and balloons into a puffer fish!
"Aw," Fluttershy coos.
"This is amazing!" Twilight exclaims.

Everyfish is having so much fun!

Princess Skystar has an idea. "You can stay with us **FOREVER**!" she says.

The ponies stop what they're doing. "That sounds lovely, darling, but you must realize we can't stay," Rarity says.

"We have to get back to our families," Applejack explains.

Princess Skystar is sad. She doesn't want her new friends to leave, but she knows they have to. "Of course. It's probably for the best. I'll just get Mom to turn you back so you can go home." She swims away.

The Seaponies float in silence. "I know we have to go, but couldn't we stay for just a little longer?" Pinkie Pie asks her friends.

"Yeah! Let's show Skystar the best time ever!" Twilight Sparkle agrees.

The group finds Princess Skystar sitting with her friends Shelly and Sheldon. "Don't be sad!" Pinkie Pie shouts. "We've got a little time to play. Let's pick one small thing to do."

"All right!" Skystar says.

Everypony wants to squeeze in as much fun with Princess Skystar as possible! Singing and dancing help brighten everypony's mood.

The Seaponies decide to make some jewelry.
They make shell necklaces for everyfish they can.
Rarity is impressed with all the unique designs!

After they finish crafting, they play a quick game of hide-and-seek. Skystar has never played before, but she's a natural.

The new friends are having so much fun. But Pinkie Pie knows there's one thing that can make a good day even better—**a party**! Everyfish is invited to join in the celebration!

Princess Skystar is enjoying the **best day ever**! Even though Twilight Sparkle, Pinkie Pie, Rainbow Dash, Applejack, Fluttershy, Rarity, and Spike can't stay Seaponies forever, Skystar knows they will always be friends.